Etched in
CLAY

Etched in
CLAY

The Life of Dave, Enslaved Potter and Poet

ANDREA CHENG

woodcuts by the author

LEE & LOW BOOKS INC.

NEW YORK

Etched in Clay is true to the known facts of Dave's life, although there are some discrepancies among sources about dates and details. The story is a narrative biography, told in verse, with some imagined scenes, people, thoughts, and dialogue. These parts of the story are dramatic extensions of historically documented events and interactions. While the language used by both white characters and enslaved African American characters in nineteenth-century South Carolina has been standardized for modern readers, Dave's inscriptions are included in their original form.

Dave's inscriptions from CAROLINA CLAY: THE LIFE AND LEGEND OF THE SLAVE POTTER DAVE by Leonard Todd. Copyright © 2008 by Leonard Todd. Used by permission of W. W. Norton & Company, Inc.

Text and illustrations copyright © 2013 by Andrea Cheng
LEE & LOW BOOKS Inc., 95 Madison Avenue, New York, NY 10016
leeandlow.com
Manufactured in the United States of America
Printed on paper from responsible sources
Book design by Christy Hale
Book production by The Kids at Our House
The text is set in Book Antigua
The illustrations are rendered as woodcuts
(hc) 10 9 8 7 6 5 4 3
(pb) 10 9 8 7 6 5 4 3 2
First Edition
Library of Congress Cataloging-in-Publication Data
Cheng, Andrea.
Etched in clay : the life of Dave, enslaved potter and poet / Andrea Cheng ; woodcuts by the author. — 1st ed.
          p. cm.
Summary: "The life of Dave, an enslaved potter who inscribed his works with sayings and poems in spite of South Carolina's slave anti-literacy laws in the years leading up to the Civil War. Includes afterword, author's note, and sources" — Provided by publisher.
ISBN 978-1-60060-451-5 (hardcover : alk. paper)   ISBN 978-1-60060-893-3 (e-book)
ISBN 978-1-62014-807-5 (paperback)
1. Dave, fl. 1834-1864 — Juvenile literature. 2. African American potters —
Biography — Juvenile literature. 3. African American poet — Biography —
Juvenile literature. 4. Slaves — South Carolina — Biography — Juvenile literature.
[1. Dave, fl. 1834-1864. 2. African American potters. 3. African American poets.
4. Slaves — South Carolina.] I. Title.
NK4210.D247C54 2012
738.092 — dc23   [B]   2012027280

To Ann

Contents

HISTORICAL RECORDS SHOW that the first
documentation of ownership of an enslaved young
man known as Dave is a mortgage agreement dated
June 13, 1818. This agreement indicates that Dave
was about seventeen years old and was owned by
Harvey Drake. Most likely, Drake purchased Dave
at a slave auction in Augusta, Georgia, prior to
1818 and took him to Pottersville, a village outside
Edgefield, South Carolina, where Drake and his
uncles — the Landrum brothers — had a stoneware
pottery business. Eventually Dave was taught how
to make pots, jugs, and jars on a potter's wheel;
fire them; and glaze them using the Landrums'
famous alkaline glazes. Soon Dave became one of
the best potters in the Edgefield district. Here is his
inspiring story.

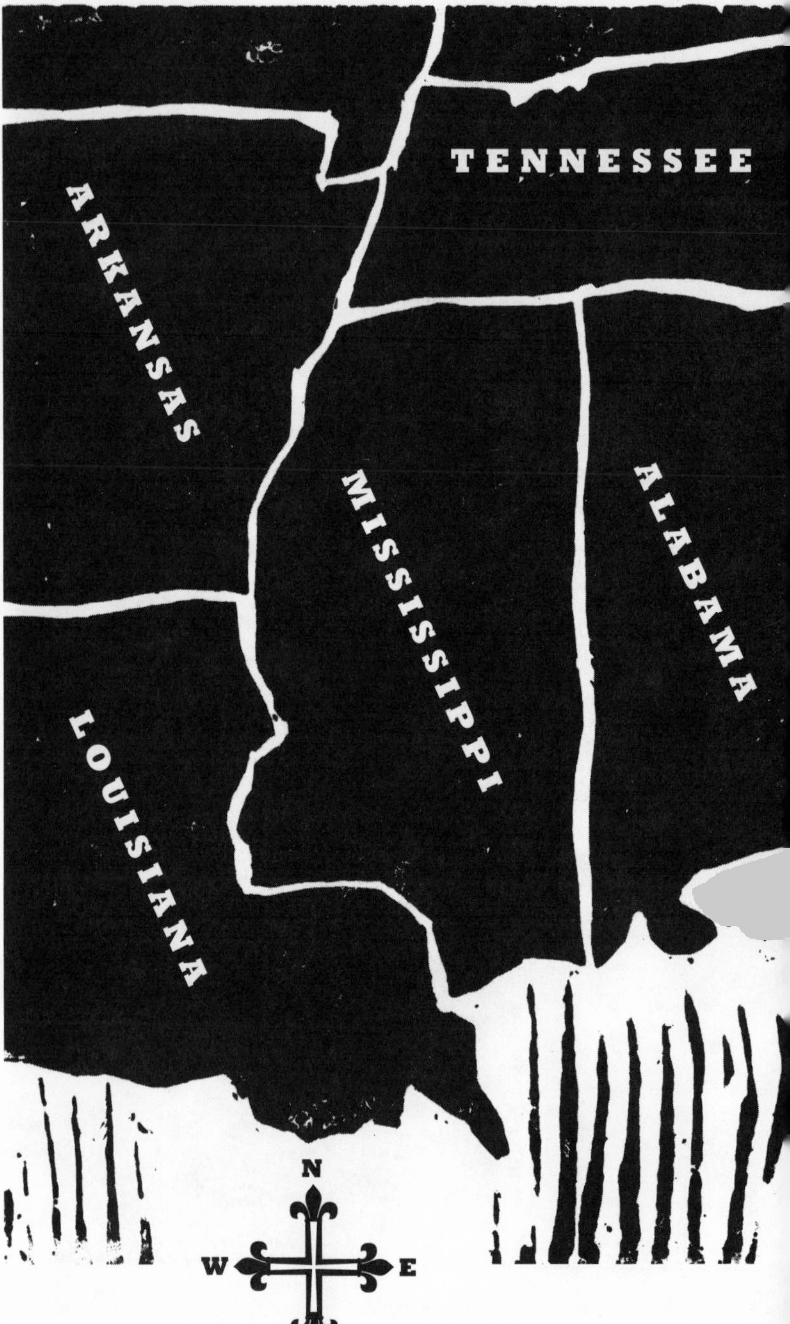

TENNESSEE

ARKANSAS

MISSISSIPPI

ALABAMA

LOUISIANA

N
W E
S

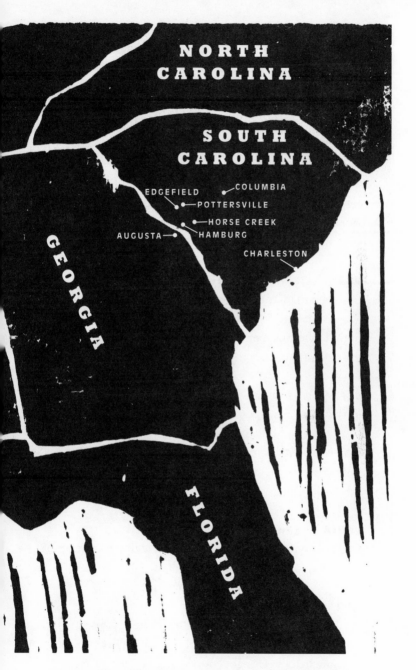

This map shows the relative locations of places important in Dave's life. Stony Bluff, which was in the vicinity of Pottersville and Horse Creek, is not indicated. Its location is known only to a few researchers, and the precise spot has not been revealed.

Main Narrators and Characters

DR. ABNER LANDRUM (1785–1859)

Around 1810, with his brother Amos, founded Pottersville Stoneware Manufactory, a pottery works located outside the town of Edgefield, South Carolina; founder of a newspaper called *The Edgefield Hive.*

HARVEY DRAKE (1796–1832)

Nephew of Dr. Abner Landrum and partner in Pottersville Stoneware Manufactory; first known owner of Dave, from sometime before 1818 until 1832.

DAVE (LATER NAMED DAVID DRAKE) (1801–LATE 1870S)

Enslaved man, country born (born in the United States); by age seventeen owned by Harvey Drake; later sold several times to various members of Drake's extended family over the next fifty years.

ELIZA (1799–DEATH DATE UNKNOWN)

Enslaved woman, possibly Dave's first wife.

SARAH DRAKE (BIRTH AND DEATH DATES UNKNOWN)

Wife of Harvey Drake; deeply spiritual member of the Edgefield Village Baptist Church.

LYDIA (BIRTH AND DEATH DATES UNKNOWN)

Enslaved woman, possibly Dave's second wife; mother of two boys, John and George.

NULLIFIER

Person who opposed the Union (the United States government) and felt that each state had the right to nullify, or veto, any measure that the U.S. government tried to impose on it.

REUBEN DRAKE (1800–SOMETIME IN THE 1850s)
Brother of Harvey Drake; purchased Dave after Harvey's death and owned Dave in Pottersville until about 1836.

HENRY SIMKINS (BIRTH AND DEATH DATES UNKNOWN)
Enslaved man who worked with Dave at the pottery works in Pottersville, Horse Creek, and Stony Bluff.

REV. JOHN LANDRUM (1765–1846)
Brother of Dr. Abner Landrum and Amos Landrum; purchased Dave to work at his pottery works in Horse Creek; owned Dave from about 1836 until 1846.

BENJAMIN FRANKLIN LANDRUM (1811–1880)
Son of Rev. John Landrum and brother of Mary Landrum Miles; built his own pottery works in another part of Horse Creek and owned Dave from 1847 until about 1849.

MARY LANDRUM MILES (1812–1877)
Daughter of Rev. John Landrum and wife of Lewis Miles.

LEWIS MILES (1808–1869)
Son-in-law of Rev. John Landrum and husband of Mary Landrum Miles; Rev. Landrum lent him Dave to work at his own pottery works in Horse Creek; later built a pottery works in Stony Bluff and owned Dave from about 1849 until the end of the Civil War in 1865.

Etched in
CLAY

Pottersville Stoneware Manufactory

DR. ABNER LANDRUM, 1810

Near Edgefield I found
the perfect place.
The forest is thick
with maples and oaks.
Streams run like veins
through the South Carolina clay,
smooth and deep red
with pockets of white.
Someday soon
our slaves will stand
knee-deep in the water,
digging clay
from the banks
while the wagon drivers wait.
We'll have one strong mule
at the mill
to turn the post
and grind the clay,
and a turning house
with potter's wheels.
We'll stoke up the fire
in our furnace
and bake our pots hot
to melt the glaze.
Should we call ourselves

Landrum Brothers Pottery?
No, too ordinary
for the finest jugs and jars
in all the land!
Allow me to introduce
our soon-to-be
world-famous
Pottersville Stoneware Manufactory.

Pottersville Partners

DR. ABNER LANDRUM, 1814

My older brother Amos
is a salesman
through and through,
but his love of drink
and the ladies
distracts him from
our business.
Let me also ask my nephew
Harvey Drake
to lend a hand.
Weak of body
but sound of mind,
he is a thoughtful man,
and prudent too.

Augusta Auction

HARVEY DRAKE, 1815

My uncle did not send me to the market
for peaches or green beans or squash.
I make my way to the auction block
crowded with people,
watching.
The Negro mothers wail
while their children cling to them
like melons to their vines.
One slave stands alone,
young but not a child,
strong enough to haul the clay
up the slippery, steep banks
of the stream.
"See here, Young Master,"
shouts the auctioneer.
"He's only six hundred dollars,
country born,
good teeth,
straight back.
Come see for yourself."
I could get two for that price,
three hundred each.
"Can you work, boy?" I ask.
"Yes, Master,
I sure can work."
There's intelligence in those eyes,

considering.
"Four hundred is all I have,"
I tell the auctioneer.
"Five hundred firm," he insists.
Others are watching
to see what I'll do.
That boy stares at me,
waiting
in the Georgia sun
while our clay is washing downstream
fast as water runs.
"Boy," I say,
"you come with me."

Another Name

DAVE, 1815

Master says, "Dave —
that suits you.
That's your name."
He can call me
whatever he pleases,
Tom or John or Will or Dave,
no matter.

I had another name once.
I can't remember the sound of it;
but I know the voice,
smooth and soft,
that whispered it
close to my ear
in the still night.
And then
my mother was gone.

Clay and Hope

DAVE, 1817

The water's cold;
my hands are ice,
even in spring.
"Dig it out now, Dave.
You can carry more clay
than that,"
Master Drake says.
Every day I dig,
I lift,
I haul,
I hope
for something else
tomorrow.

Pottery Lesson

DAVE, 1819

I sit by the door
of the turning house
and watch Master Drake
form our clay
into a jar,
wide in the middle,
narrow on top,
his hands steady
while he kicks the wheel
at the bottom,
making the upper wheel turn
faster and faster.
He adds water,
then pulls up the sides
of the jar,
shaping and trimming —
like magic.

"Are you staring at me, Dave?"
"No, Master," I say.
"Do you want to learn
to turn a pot?"
"Yes, Master."
"Get up here, boy."
"Right now?" I ask.
"I'm waiting," he says.

I scramble to my feet.
"Balance your weight,
now kick the bottom wheel
and center the mound.
Keep that wheel spinning.
You got it, boy.
Put your thumb in the middle
and squeeze."

In my hands
the clay comes to life,
growing so quick,
like a weed in the rain.
Master Drake is watching.
Then he says,
"Looks like
you may have talent, Dave."

My heart starts beating so fast
I can hardly breathe.
Slow and steady,
I draw that jar right up.

Dangerous Talent
HARVEY DRAKE, 1820

Others take six months
to learn to center
a mound on the wheel,
but in just two weeks,
Dave gets the feel
of the clay.
He pins his elbows
to his sides,
then cups his hands
to hold the clay.
Knuckle on the outside,
he brings up the walls
of a gallon jar
with the lip turned out
just right.
Then I show him
how to roll thick handles
and mount them
on the sides.

Dave is smiling
like I gave him gold.
And I wonder,
Is there danger in teaching
this slave boy so much?
Will he forget his place?

Jumping the Broomstick

"What's the matter, Eliza?"
Master Drake asks.
"Our Dave isn't good enough
for you to marry?"
He's younger than I like,
only nineteen,
and skinny too;
but with that wheel,
he can turn out a jar
faster than I can wash it.
He's kind too,
except on rare occasions,
when he drinks.

I put on my dress,
blue as the sky,
with white dots like cotton
ripe in the fields.
Dave is standing there
in black pants
and white shirt.
We jump the broomstick,
and the minister says
we'll be together
"till death or distance
do you part."

"Sweet Eliza,"
Dave whispers.
He kisses me
on the cheek,
and I take his hand.

You Should Be Grateful

HARVEY DRAKE, 1821

She ought to be glad
she's a house slave
and not picking cotton
under the burning sun
from dawn to dusk.
But no,
Eliza wants to stay in that shack
with her Dave.
Hey, girl,
didn't anyone ever teach you
to be grateful for what you have?
You've got food to fill you up,
a dry roof over your head.
What else do you want?
I've seen Dave's eyes on you
every time you pass.
Isn't that enough
to make you smile?

My Eliza

DAVE, 1822

My Eliza —
sometimes
like a cat
she sneaks into the shack
late at night.
She rubs my back,
so tired
from bending over the wheel.
She kneads my tight muscle,
making it soft
like fresh-dug clay.
We breathe deep,
and for a while,
alone in our shack
away from the turning house
and the Big House,
we feel safe.

That Man Is Mine

ELIZA, 1824

Master Drake thinks
working in the Big House
is better than picking cotton
in the fields.
What does he know?
I wash and press
mountains of clothes.
I scrub the floors
and scour the pots.
I cut up baskets of onions
till tears run down
my face.
And the Mistress
always watching,
never leaving me alone.

Then out the window
I see Dave
carrying a great big jug,
the muscles in his arms
rippling,
and I think —
That man is mine.

I Beg You

DAVE, 1825

I heard it said
Master Drake has some intention
of selling Eliza.
Could be a rumor,
you know how people talk.
But I heard him say Alabama
and Eliza's name.

I run down to the turning house.
Master Drake is mixing slip,
the watery clay
that glues the handles
onto our jars.
"Please, Master," I say,
"I beg you with all my heart.
Let Eliza stay,
or send me with her."
"Can't you see I'm busy, Dave?"
"Yes, Master, but I beg you —"
"Go on back now.
It's getting late.
What would a potter slave
like you
do in Alabama anyway,
where there are
no pottery works?"

At night I listen
to the crickets and frogs.
What's that rustling?
Could someone be packing up
to go?
I'm afraid to sleep
for fear come morning
Eliza will be gone.

Departure

ELIZA, 1825

The minister said,
"Till death or *distance*
do you part."
Could it be he knew?
Master Drake says,
"Come on, Eliza.
Walk with the wagon now."
I ask if I can say
good-bye to Dave,
but Master Drake just laughs.
"No need, Eliza.
They'll find you another man
real quick."
He winks —
and I cry.

Brilliant Glazes

DR. ABNER LANDRUM, 1825

Elegant porcelain
I failed to make.
But my glazes
for stoneware pottery
are the finest
in all the land.
No need
for expensive salt
or poisonous lead.
My glazes are made
from wood ash,
sand,
a little clay;
grind them fine,
add water,
mix.
And when the fire's roaring hot
my glazes melt smooth as glass,
brilliant
in the Carolina sun.

Loading the Furnace

DR. ABNER LANDRUM, 1826

Little John, you crawl inside
and start loading up
the furnace.
Be careful, boy.
No pot or jar is to touch another one,
you hear?
Tom and Jack,
Dan and Dave,
you boys split these logs,
make slabs long and narrow
to fuel the fire.
Dave, did you dip that big bowl
in glaze for me like I said?
Then keep splitting those logs,
because we're firing hot
tomorrow.

Firing Time

DR. ABNER LANDRUM, 1826

Early in the morning,
we stoke the fire
slow at first,
letting the sides
of the furnace heat up.
Soon the neighboring folks
come out to watch,
children running all around
and underfoot.

"Come on now, boys," I say.
"Take the fire up quick.
Stuff those slabs in
as fast as you can."

The furnace is roaring
louder than thunder,
a ball of fire
turning my glazes
blue
and green
and yellow
bright as gold.
Finally the orange flame
leaps out of the chimney.
"You've done it, boys!" I shout.

The children cheer,
their mothers smile,
and the smoke lingers
in the air
for hours.

What's Gotten into That Boy?

DR. ABNER LANDRUM, 1826

Dave is the only one
not smiling.
I don't know
what's gotten into that boy.
"Dave, take that frown
off your face," I say.
"Yes, Master."
"Do you have a problem today?"
"No, Master."
"Then you smile, hear?"
"Yes, Master."
Almost a year's gone by.
Could he still be missing
that bony girl,
the one Harvey sold
to those folks
heading for Alabama?

That's My Jar

It takes three days
for the furnace to cool.
Even before the sun comes up
on the last day,
I smell the ash.
Little John and me,
we climb the hill
to the furnace.
Doctor Landrum and Master Drake
are already there.
Doctor Landrum's voice is clear.
"Morning, boys," he says.
"You ready?"

I unbrick the door.
Little John hands me the jars
one by one,
warm and shining
in the rising sun.
Doctor Landrum says,
"See that green?
Have you ever seen a color
shimmer like that?"
He holds my jar,
the big one with the lip
and glaze dripping

down the sides.
"Now, that's a jar,"
he says,
forgetting it was me
who dug the clay,
and centered the mound,
and pushed my weight
against the wheel,
forgetting it was me
who rolled the clay
for the handles
thick and solid.
See the thumbprints
on the sides?
Those are from my hands.

We line up the jars and jugs
by the road
for all of South Carolina
to come and see our wares.
Whoever buys the big one
will never know
I made that jar.

The Scriptures

SARAH DRAKE, 1826

Every morning
I read the words
of the Scriptures.
It is up to each and every sinner
to search the Scriptures
for himself
until he finds salvation
in the words of the Lord.
How, may I ask,
are slaves to search
unless they know their letters?

My dear husband,
take this little spelling book
and leave it with Dave
in the hope
that it will help him
find a way
to learn his letters
and someday
read the message
of our Lord.

Our Conscience

HARVEY DRAKE, 1826

No doubt,
my dear wife,
we are bound
by our conscience
and our beliefs.
Dave learns fast.
In a matter of months
I'm sure he will master
the basics of reading
with this spelling book.
Just be forewarned —
while allowing our slaves
to read is our duty,
teaching them to write
is punishable
by South Carolina law.
Writing is a dangerous tool.
A slave who writes
might forge a pass to freedom
or conspire with others
to organize a revolt.
Indeed, writing
is a weapon.

The Blue Back Speller

DAVE, 1827

A small book it is
but big of heart,
for with Mr. Webster's
blue book
I am learning to read.
I stare at the pages,
struggling to make sense
of the letters,
until one day
they jump off the page!

One-syllable words:
pig,
man,
dog,
horse.

Two-syllable words:
Mas-ter,
pot-ter,
Edge-field.

I should blow out
the candle,
save the wax,
but I've turned

to the long words
that I love best:
mag-nan-i-mous,
sa-gac-i-ty,
se-ver-i-ty.

Here is one
I had never heard:
con-cat-e-na-tion.
What does it mean?
"Chains," Doctor Landrum said,
"a linking together."
Like the chains of bondage,
the shackles around the legs
of us slaves.
Mr. Webster,
it seems to me
we know each other.

Tell the World
DAVE, APRIL 18, 1827

Master Drake sees me
take paper scraps
to practice my letters.
He clears his throat.
"A slave who can read
is one thing,
but a slave who can write
is a menace,
causing trouble for himself
and others," he says.

I'm alone in the shed
making bricks all day
until my back
is about to break.
Put clay in the mold,
scrape off the excess,
let it set,
turn it out.
Four bricks at a time,
hundreds by noon,
each one the same
as the rest.

How is writing letters
and words

a menace?
This stick here
is sharp and straight,
just right for carving words
in wet clay.
I'll put the date —
April 18 —
on the backs
of these bricks
to tell the world
that on this day
a man started practicing
his letters.

The Edgefield Hive

DR. ABNER LANDRUM, 1828

What's a town
without a newspaper?
The Edgefield Hive,
now that's a name
for sure,
a journal swarming
with ideas.
My dear nephews,
Harvey and Reuben,
the pottery manufactory is yours
while I use my paper
to tell our citizens
of the sciences and arts.
I'll need someone to help me
haul the paper
and clean the press.
Would be better
if he could read.
Why of course —
Dave,
the potter slave.

Real Paper, Real Ink

DAVE, 1830

Carry the newsprint,
oil the levers
of the printing press,
clean the handles
covered with ink.
After *The Hive* is printed,
I put the letters,
one by one,
back into their places,
to be pulled out again
for tomorrow's words.
So many words
five and six syllables long:
corporosity,
compressibility,
incivility.

By the time my work
is done,
the light outside
is fading.
But now it's my turn
to copy words
onto real paper with real ink,
over and over,
until my hand is too tired

to hold the pen
and my eyes start closing
as I write.

Late at night
in my shack,
I toss and turn on my cot.
The air is so still
it's hard to breathe.
I miss the potter's wheel
and the coolness of clay
on my skin.
I miss Eliza's warm hands
rubbing my back.
I sit up
and write a letter
in my head:
My dearest Eliza,
Please know
your husband is missing you
each and every day
and with these words
he is sending you
his love.

Education

ENSLAVED CHILD, 1830

Uncle Dave,
you going to teach us some more
today?
We got our sticks.
We're ready.

He takes my stick,
and in the dirt he writes:
dog,
cat,
pig,
cow.

We're tired of those baby words!

"Keep your voice down,"
Uncle Dave warns.
"You know this learning
can get us in trouble
if we're not careful."

Okay, Uncle Dave.
We'll talk quiet.
But can you give us
a word
with lots of letters?

Ed-u-ca-tion, he writes.
What's that?

"It's what you're doing
right now — learning,"
Uncle Dave says.
"It's reading and writing
and thinking."

After everyone's gone home,
Uncle Dave reads me a story
from Mr. Webster's spelling book
about good boys
who want to learn.
One day
I'm going to read that story
by myself.

A New Husband

LYDIA, 1830

I feel Dave watching me
when I walk past.
He's a smart man,
I know that,
with all those big words
pouring out of his mouth.

Dave had a wife once
when he was a young man.
She's gone now,
sold off
before his eyes.

I had a husband once.
I can see his face
in both my sons.
He's gone now too,
sold off
before *my* eyes.

Dave wants to marry me,
and I'm thinking
it's hard to raise these boys
alone.
The boys have taken to Dave.
He is teaching George and John
to read,
and John likes to climb
into Dave's lap at night.

The broomstick is waiting,
and I will jump.

Submissionists

A NULLIFIER, 1831

Good people of South Carolina,
there are some
in our dear nation
who are determined
to destroy the heart and soul
of the South.
First the government takes
our money.
Next it will order us
to free our slaves.
We will always and forever
oppose taxes and tariffs
and threats to the institutions
that Southern states hold dear.
Unionists,
is that what they call themselves?
They claim to protect our nation.
Blundering, bumbling submissionists,
that's what I say they are!
We will create our own government
in the South
before we will ever submit
and let the Unionists
have their way.

Speaking Out

DR. ABNER LANDRUM, 1831

As a defender of the Union,
I can no longer stay in Edgefield,
where the Nullifiers surround me
and drown out my voice.
Don't misunderstand me;
I am not against the South.
But this country is one,
and I must speak out more forcefully
for the Unionist cause.
Columbia, the capital of our state,
beckons me
to defend our land with words.
I will send copies
of my renamed newspaper,
The Columbia Free Press and Hive,
to Harvey Drake
for all in Edgefield and Pottersville
to read,
so they may know
that the Constitution of the United States
will stand forever.

Dave,
you will go back
to the pottery works,
and while your hands

are wet with clay,
remember this:
a man must stand up
for what he thinks is right
even when
he stands alone.

Words and Verses

DAVE, 1831

Several times a week
Master Drake brings
The Columbia Free Press and Hive
to the turning house.
I read Doctor Landrum's
words and verses
for all to hear.
"He reads nice,"
one of the other potters says,
surprised
that I know my letters
and can read
Doctor Landrum's big words.

All day long
I'm turning pots and jars
on the potter's wheel
while *my* words and verses
swirl in my head.
But what's a verse
if it can't be read?

Someday
I'll write down verses of my own
and sign my name:
Dave.

Death of Harvey Drake

DR. ABNER LANDRUM, 1832

There was no better man
in all the land
than Harvey Drake.
Gripped by a fever
at the age of thirty-six,
my nephew died too young.
He leaves a wife
without a husband,
children
without a father,
and slaves
without a master.
He leaves scores of pots
unturned,
the clay a wet mound
of potential.

Lord, Help Us

DAVE, 1832

Why didn't Master Drake
leave a will?
I know that means
the auction block is waiting.
The voice of the auctioneer,
I remember it well.
"He's country born,
good teeth,
straight back."
Now my back aches
from working clay,
and two teeth
are gone out of my mouth.
I have Lydia and her boys,
who are old enough
to be sold away
to work.

The boys, afraid to sleep,
cling to their mother
like baby possums.
Could this be our last night
together?
I rub their backs,
first John, then George.
Go to sleep, boys,

go to sleep.
Lydia sits close to me
and reaches for my hand.

Lord, help us
and keep us together,
for we have lost too much
in this world
already.

Purchase

REUBEN DRAKE, 1833

Four hundred dollars
to purchase Dave?
More than I anticipated,
but what choice do I have?
My brother is dead,
but still we have
the clay and the wood,
the water and the furnace.
And now Dave will continue
to turn the potter's wheel.
In the name of my brother,
Harvey Drake,
Pottersville Stoneware Manufactory
will live on.

Missing Dave

LYDIA, 1833

Oh, thank goodness!
My boys are still with me.
They are saying
how much they miss Dave,
and I say
they could be missing Mama too.
We could have been sold separate,
to plantations far away,
instead of being bought
by Master Drake's widow.
Then my tears start falling
and won't stop.
I don't know why I'm crying
when Dave's with Reuben Drake,
only a mile
down the road.
Truth is,
I want him here
with me.

Second Nature

DAVE, 1833

Centering a mound of clay
is like walking.
Once you learn to do it,
you never forget.
You let your body settle in,
relaxed but firm.
Don't fight the clay
because it's sure to win,
landing like a heap of mud
at your feet.
See here;
you lean in,
elbows down,
no flopping like a fish.
And once the mound is centered,
you draw the walls up,
shaping things
the way you want,
wide mouth or narrow,
thin walls or thick.
To some it looks like magic,
but to me,
making a jar
is second nature.

Nat Turner

DAVE, 1834

Nat Turner — I heard
he was a brave man,
led a rebellion of slaves
up in Virginia.
He knew his Scriptures,
knew God was telling him
to set slaves free.
So when a sign
came from the sky
and the sun almost disappeared
during the day,
the time was right.
More than fifty whites killed
in a single day,
one single day.
Nat Turner was hanged
for leading this rebellion,
but I'm telling you,
Mr. Turner,
you were a braver man
than I.

End Slave Literacy

A NULLIFIER, 1834

David Walker in Boston,
Nat Turner in Virginia,
stirring up the slaves
these past few years,
killing white men,
innocent women,
and children too.
It's just plain wrong,
and we have had enough!
People, you must understand
that when you teach a slave
to read and write,
you are giving him the tools
to send out a message
and plan his escape —
or worse,
to slit your throat.
Let us pass a law
here in South Carolina:
a slave who learns to write
will be given twenty lashes,
and his teacher will pay
a hefty fine.

Etched in Clay

Only me here,
turning pots, making jars,
turning words inside my head
until I'm ready to explode
like a jar with an air bubble
in the furnace.

Magnanimous,
sagacity,
concatenation.
Here, on this jar
for all to see,
I'll inscribe the date,
June 12, 1834,
and the word
Concatination.
Someday the world will read
my word etched in clay
on the side of this jar
and know about the shackles
around our legs
and the whips
upon our backs.
I am not afraid
to write on a jar
and fire it hot

so my word
can never be erased.
And if some day
this jar cracks,
my word will stay,
etched in the shards.

A Poem!

DAVE, JULY 12, 1834

The summer's so hot,
it's like we're living
in the furnace.
The clay doesn't like it either,
getting hard on me
too quick.
I better hurry now,
before the sun's too low to see.
What words will I scrawl
across the shoulder
of this jar?
I hear Lydia's voice in my head.
Be careful, Dave.
Those words in clay
can get you killed.
But I will die of silence
if I keep my words inside me
any longer.
Doctor Landrum used to say
it's best to write a poem a day,
for it calms the body
and the soul
to shape those words.

This jar is a beauty,
big and wide,

fourteen gallons
I know it will hold.
I have the words now,
and my stick is sharp.
I write:
put every bit all between
surely this Jar will hold 14.

Anti-Literacy Law

MEMBER OF SOUTH CAROLINA GENERAL ASSEMBLY,
DECEMBER 17, 1834

New law, passed today by the
South Carolina General Assembly:
Any white person
convicted of teaching a slave
to read or write
will be fined up to one hundred dollars
and put in prison for up to six months.
Any slave
convicted of teaching another slave
to read or write
will get fifty lashes.
Any informers
will receive half the money collected
from the fines.

Stop That Foolishness

LYDIA, 1835

If I ever catch you again
with that little spelling book
I'll tan your hide.
You hear me, George?
You hear me, John?
No more reading and writing.
If somebody tells somebody
who tells somebody else,
they'll take you
and cut off your fingers
so you won't ever write again.
You want five fingers
on each hand?
Then you better stop
that foolishness.
If you don't,
they're sure to hurt you,
and make you tell them
Dave gave you that book,
and then they'll whip him bloody.
Is that what you want?

Delivery

REUBEN DRAKE, 1835

Dave,
you and Little John
load these pots and jars
into the wagon.
Then you, Dave,
drive it all the way
to the railroad depot
in Hamburg
so our pottery may be sent
to towns across the state.
Tomorrow, bring me back
the supplies we need
and a keg of rum.
Here's the money, Dave.
Keep it safe.
I'll be checking that keg
when you get back
to make sure it's full.
Well, what are you waiting for?
Get to work, boys.

On the Train Tracks

PASSENGER ON TRAIN FROM CHARLESTON
TO COLUMBIA, 1835

Feeling sick on the train,
I think to look out the front,
and what do I see
but someone upon the tracks.
"Stop! Stop!
Stop the engine!"
The train jolts to a halt
too late.
There lay a Negro man and his leg,
the blood flowing into the gravel,
the bone cut in two.
A stranger hauls him up,
says he's heavy too,
and ties the wound with rags.
We hear him moan,
calling for his mother,
and then he is silent.
I don't know what happened
after that,
but I suspect he was dead.

Turning, Turning

DAVE, 1835

The wheels of the train,
turning, turning,
like the clay on the wheel,
turning, turning.
Oh, the stars were so bright
that night
and more than I had ever seen.
It's coming back to me now.
I had been to Hamburg
to sell our wares.
Reuben Drake said
bring back the rum keg
full to the brim.
In the dark,
I filled my small flask,
filled it three times,
a small treat
on a cool night.

I lay down on the tracks
to see those stars,
the constellations forming messages
to my mother
and Eliza and Lydia
and George and John —
long words

scrawled across the heavens.
I heard a whistle
from far away
and thought
my mother was calling.

Now I have one leg.

Letter to Dave

DR. ABNER LANDRUM, 1835

Take heart, Dave.
Hamburg is not so far
from here.
Soon as you are well enough
we'll send for you.
Lydia and the boys are waiting,
as am I.
Remember,
Josiah Wedgwood had but one leg
and he made the finest pottery
in all the world.
Get well, Dave.

Very truly yours,
Dr. Abner Landrum

Home Again

True to his word,
Doctor Landrum brings me home.
Lydia, John, and George
are waiting
under the hackberry tree
trying not to stare
at the stump
that was my leg.
"Does it hurt?" John asks.
I nod.
How can it be
that I feel pain
in a leg
that is gone?

On to Louisiana

SARAH DRAKE, 1836

With my husband gone,
I am moving west
to a new state
and a new life.

"Hurry now," I say.
"Lydia, George, John,
we have a long way to go
before dark.
You can move faster
than that."

See how she cries,
so sad to leave Dave.
Lydia knows Dave is not mine,
and a one-legged man
cannot walk to Louisiana.
Even if he rode in the wagon,
Louisiana is no place
for a potter.
There's no clay there,
no pottery works.
Lydia knows this,
but she doesn't quite seem
to understand.

Why?
DAVE, 1836

Lydia and the boys,
Eliza,
my mother —
all gone.
Why, Lord,
do you leave me alone?
I know
I have the stars
outside my window
like thousands of lights
sparkling in the night.
Long ago my mother told me
you are never alone
while you're watching the stars.
That's what she said.
But why, Lord,
with all these stars,
do I still feel
all alone?

A Helper

Henry Simkins
has crippled arms that hang useless,
like shirtsleeves on the wash line,
but his legs are strong.
Henry is here
to turn the wheel for me.
Who knows?
My two good hands
to shape the clay
plus his two good legs
to kick the wheel
might work out
some kind of way.

Carving Words

DAVE, MARCH 29, 1836

The clay is soft,
the stick in my hand is sharp.
Carefully I carve my poem
deep into the shoulder
of my jar:
horses mules and hogs —
all our cows is in the bogs —
there they shall ever stay
till the buzzards take them away =

A poem is a valuable thing,
for every word
means more than it says.
I know I could be whipped,
or hung from the nearest tree,
for writing these words.
Let them punish me.
Then who will mold their jars?
To our masters we are just
horses, mules, and hogs
working until we die.
But when I write,
I am a man.

Our Legacy

REV. JOHN LANDRUM, 1836

Pottersville is shrinking
like a shriveled peach
in the summer sun.
Harvey Drake has passed,
and his brother, Reuben,
is going west to Louisiana.
Still, here at my pottery works
in Horse Creek
our legacy lives on.
The clay is fresh and waiting.
My brother Abner
has sent me his recipes
for the finest glazes
in all the land,
scientifically developed,
tried and true.
And Reuben will sell me
his one-legged potter, Dave,
to turn our pots and jugs and jars.

The Landrum brothers
will remain
a family of potters.

Horse Creek

DAVE, 1836

Reverend Landrum has me sit
in the wagon
since my hobbling
on a crutch
is mighty slow.
Good-bye, Pottersville.
Good-bye, Edgefield,
with your courthouse standing tall.
Good-bye, my friends
and relations.
We're finding new clay
downstream
in a place called Horse Creek.
Henry Simkins,
with his crippled arms,
is coming too,
to turn the potter's wheel
for me.

A Loan

REV. JOHN LANDRUM, 1839

Not brilliant, perhaps,
this son-in-law of mine,
but Lewis Miles is kind,
and he loves my daughter, Mary,
from the bottom of his heart.
Lewis wants to learn
the pottery business too.
For a modest fee
I will send him Dave,
the potter slave,
to show him how
to throw a pot on the wheel
and mix the famous
Landrum glazes.
With the help of Lewis Miles,
another pottery works
in Horse Creek
will grow and thrive.

Luck Is Here

LEWIS MILES, 1839

Who would believe
that my father-in-law
has lent Dave to me
to shape the jugs and jars
at my own pottery works?
I am not yet skilled,
and the clay is lifeless
in my hands.
But learning does not happen
overnight,
and I have time.
Luck is here with me
at Horse Creek,
where I found my love
and my life.

I Made This Jar

DAVE, JANUARY 27, 1840

He is a generous man,
this Lewis Miles,
giving money to every beggar,
more than what is even asked.
On my jars
made in his turning house,
I'll put his name
with a fancy *M*,
and I'll write my name too:
Dave.
They gave me this name,
so can I not use it?
This jar is mine.
I made it
with my two good hands.
I made this jar.

A Master Potter

LEWIS MILES, 1840

Dave has but one leg,
yet I have never seen anyone
make a jar so big
and strong
and handsome.
He shows me how to draw
the jar up slow,
knuckle bent,
taking each ring of clay
a little at a time.
Then when the clay
cannot be thinner,
we let it set.
"The sun is low," I tell Dave.
"Time to eat."
He shakes his head.
"I still have work to do."
"When you're done," I say,
"there's soup waiting at the house."
I leave him there alone,
a potter like no other,
and a patient teacher too.
Sometimes I forget
Dave's skin is black.

This Jar Is Bare

DAVE, JULY 13, 1840

I know it's late,
but this big jar
is looking bare.
What should I write
across the top?
My stomach growls,
and I can smell the soup
boiling at the house.
I pick up my stick and write:
Dave belongs to Mr Miles /
wher the oven bakes & the pot biles ///
Then I set the jar on the shelf,
take my crutch,
and hobble up the hill
for dinner.

To Lewis Miles

REV. JOHN LANDRUM, 1841

My dear son-in-law,
have you heard the news?
In Augusta a group of slaves —
and mind you some could
read and write —
plotted to burn down the town
and kill the residents.
Now this is serious.
You cannot continue
to be so lenient
with Dave.
You must make him
stop his writing.
Any jars and jugs found
with his words around their necks
should be shattered,
and the potter slave
whipped.

Write No More

LEWIS MILES, 1842

Dave, for many months
you have taught me here,
in the turning house,
to form our pots and jars
with handles thick
upon their sides
and glazes bright
upon their walls.
But listen.
Now it's my turn to teach.
You must put down your stick.
It is too dangerous
to let others know
you can read and write.
Your words inscribed in clay
can be no more.
You understand me, Dave?
Any pot or jar or jug
that you write on
will be destroyed.

The Choice Is Mine

DAVE, OCTOBER 13, 1843

The clay is wet
and the choice is mine.
No matter what Lewis Miles says,
I will write my letters
small and big
on this jar.
My head is not
full of verses today.
I know:
L. Miles and *Dave* —
our names —
that's all this jar
will bear.

Stubborn

LEWIS MILES, 1843

Stubborn Dave,
he continues to defy me.
I have no choice
but to smash his jar
into shards so small
no one can read
our names in the clay.
A handsome jar,
it breaks my heart
to destroy it.
I hoist the thing
above my head.
Wait.
Is there some way
to save it?
No, I cannot take the chance.
I throw the jar hard
against the wall
and listen
as it shatters.

Silence

DAVE, 1844

I center the mound of clay,
draw up a jar,
slice it off the wheel,
and set it on the shelf
to dry.
Now I am a silent potter machine.

In my head,
I cannot stop the words from flowing:
lamentable,
philanthropic,
disenfranchised,
vulnerable.
But I don't write them down,
and the words float away
like twigs in a stream,
stuck on a rock
for a moment
and then gone.

My Father's Death

MARY LANDRUM MILES, 1846

My father,
the Reverend John Landrum,
lived eighty-one years;
may his soul
rest in peace.
My husband, Lewis, says
Dave must now be ours.
He has been on
a permanent loan to us
for so many years.
But my father's will
says nothing in particular
about Dave,
and a loan
is not forever.

For Sale

LEWIS MILES, 1847

Before his death,
Reverend Landrum
did declare in his will
that when he passed on,
all his goods should be sold
and the money raised
be divided
among his kin.

Dave knows, I know,
the time is near.
He will be auctioned
on the block once more,
and I fear I do not have
enough money
to buy him.

Sold Again

DAVE, FEBRUARY 22, 1847

The auctioneer shouts,
splitting the morning air
with his voice,
splitting husbands
from their wives,
mothers
from their children,
me from Eliza,
Lydia, John, and George
long ago —
loved ones
all scattered like seeds
upon the wind.

When it's my turn,
I have no fear.
Everyone knows
my leg is gone,
but the jars I make
are big and handsome.
The auctioneer calls,
and names run
through my mind:
Harvey Drake — Doctor Landrum —
Reverend Landrum — Lewis Miles.
Surely Lewis Miles
will buy me today.
But here's Franklin,
son of the reverend.
Franklin waves a stack of bills
thicker than all the rest,
and I am his.

A High Price

BENJAMIN FRANKLIN LANDRUM, 1847

Eight hundred dollars
is a high price to pay
for a one-legged slave,
but my pottery works
can use his hands.
He's the very best potter,
white or black,
in all of Edgefield County.
My brother-in-law,
Lewis Miles,
glared at me
across the auction field.
I know he wanted Dave.
Then Lewis bought that cripple,
Henry Simkins,
as if he's the only one
who can turn the potter's wheel
for Dave.
I have a boy,
only twelve,
who can surely do that job.

Get to Work!

BENJAMIN FRANKLIN LANDRUM, 1848

That Ann,
sullen and mean,
she needs a lashing,
and I'm ready to start
today.
It takes a strong whip
to control these slaves.
Forty lashes
the Bible says.

I tell Ann to carry the pots
to the shelf
and sweep up the floor,
and she says, "I'm tired, Master."
"You are what?" I ask.
"I won't clean today," she says.
"I'll clean tomorrow."
We're in the turning house
with Dave and the rest,
their white eyeballs popping out
to see what will happen.
I raise my whip.
"You get to work
NOW!" I shout.
And when she doesn't budge,
my lash comes down

in designs
across her back.
"Get to work!" I shout again.
When she refuses,
I tie her with a rope
and leave her be.
That will make her
think about
her behavior.

Wait for Night

DAVE, 1848

A young boy kicks the wheel
and I'm throwing jar after jar,
not watching the whip come down.
But the sound —
What can we do?

The Master stomps
out of the turning house.
After his footsteps
fade on the hill,
I whisper, "Ann?"
She doesn't answer.
I know she's tied behind the wall.
"Wait for night," I say.
"I'll bring you a drink."

Must have been
she tied a brick
to one end of that rope
and threw it over the rafters.
When I bring the water,
Ann is hanging limp,
and her pulse
is gone.

Stony Bluff

LEWIS MILES, 1849

Nearby
in Stony Bluff
I've built a new pottery works
with a furnace bigger than any
in South Carolina.
But a furnace without a potter
is worth nothing.

My wife's brother, Franklin,
is a man without scruples.
Although her father's will
appointed Franklin
to manage her affairs,
Mary has demanded
that he no longer be in charge.
My brother is Mary's new trustee,
and he has requested the purchase
of one of Franklin's slaves.
That would be
Dave.

Homecoming

Working here
at this new place
in Stony Bluff
is a homecoming for me!
Lewis Miles laughs
at my jokes,
my twists of a phrase.
Henry Simkins
turns the wheel
so fast and smooth,
and the jars I shape
are enormous.
Then the words
start flowing in my head.
Once again
I pick up a writing stick.
Can I remember
how to form a *J*?
The clay is waiting,
and the memory is in my hands:
just a mammouth Jar . . .
is all I write.
For now
that is enough.

A Joke

"Dave, that handle will crack,"
Lewis Miles says,
and I say it won't.
On the top of the jar I write:
Lm says this handle
will crack.
But I'm right,
because it doesn't,
and the joke is on the jar
for all to see.

Good Times

LEWIS MILES, 1856

There is no pottery works
in all the South
as large as mine
in Stony Bluff.
Look here;
the smoke from our furnace
blows across the valley,
and people from all corners
of the land seek out
our pots and jars and jugs.
And Dave keeps writing
his messages and verses,
sending them into the world
carved in clay.

Where Is My Family?

DAVE, AUGUST 16, 1857

The sky is dark,
no stars, no moon.
How can I know
when my mother passed?
What about Eliza,
who smiled at me
as she walked by.
What about Lydia
and John and George?
Are those boys still reading
and writing?
"Please," George would beg.
"Teach us how to spell
another word."
Where are they now?
I go back to the turning house,
and by the light of a candle,
I write across my newest jar:
I wonder where is all my relation
friendship to all — and, every nation.

Our Fortune

LEWIS MILES, 1858

Like a jar cracked in two,
the country is splitting.
A war is coming
between the South and the North.
In a time of war,
our hard-earned fortune
will be worthless
if kept as paper money.
But gold and silver will endure.
I will have Dave make me
a small jar each month,
more solid than the earth.
Every month I will buy
some gold or silver
and fill a jar,
then bury it deep
in the ground.
There our fortune will stay
until our country
is at peace.

Jar of Riches

DAVE, APRIL 8, 1858

This noble jar = will hold, 20
fill it with silver = then you'll have plenty

Great and Noble Jar

DAVE, MAY 13, 1859

My jars are the envy
of every potter in the area;
wheel thrown on the bottom,
coiled clay on the top —
a method devised by me.
Lewis Miles says, "Dave,
I bet you can't make one
that holds forty gallons."
And I say, "I bet I can."
My helper rolls out ropes of clay
more than six feet long.
I coil each rope
around the bottom of the jar
and smooth the new clay
into the old
with short, clean strokes,
careful to blend the seams.
Then we turn the wheel
slow and steady,
and I shape that jar
till it reaches for the sky.
Across the top I write:
Great & Noble Jar . . . ,
for that
it truly is.

War

LEWIS MILES, 1861

The Confederate army
calls us to fight
for the South
against the Union army
from the North.
Tears flow.
"Our sons are but boys,"
my wife says,
reaching up
to kiss their cheeks
as they leave
to join the troops.
Milton,
John,
Francis —
may the Lord be with you
and keep you safe.

Our boys are eager
to go to war.
They will fight hard
for the South,
for a victory
swift and sure.
Deep in their hearts
they know

that if this war
is lost,
the slaves will be freed,
and the life
they have now
will be gone.

Repentance

DAVE, MAY 3, 1862

Another jar,
a real beauty.
On this one I write:
I, made this Jar, all of cross
If, you dont repent, you will be, lost =

Word comes of many deaths,
and at the end of the war
the guilt will lie upon this land
thick as my ropes of clay,
thick as the handles
on a forty-gallon jar.

The End Is Near

DAVE, 1864

Henry turns the wheel
with his still-strong legs.
I center the clay
and draw up the sides of a jar
like I've been doing
most every day
of my life.
Many of the other slaves
have been sent to serve
in the Confederate army
to help save Charleston.
Others saw their chance
to escape
and ran
to Union lines.

"It's quiet around here,"
Henry says.
"They'll be coming back soon,"
I say.
"How do you know?"
"I read the newspapers.
They say the end of the war
is near,
and it looks like the North
is winning."

Henry stops the wheel
from turning.
I slice off the jar
and set it on the shelf to dry.
"I sure do hope,"
Henry says,
"that by the time
all these jars
are glazed and fired
we will be free."

Black in Blue

LEWIS MILES, JUNE 21, 1865

The war between
the South and the North
is over.
The Union soldiers
who march through our town
have skin as dark as Dave's.
The sooner we sign
the oath of loyalty
to the Union,
the sooner these black soldiers
in the blue uniforms
of the North
will go back
to where they came from
and leave us to rebuild
our lives.

What Did I Expect?

LEWIS MILES, 1865

I walk slowly
down the path
full of stones
to where the slaves
are filling our furnace.
They stop and stare.

I open my mouth,
but the words are stuck.
Finally they come out
in a whisper.

"Boys," I say,
"today you,
your women,
and your children
are free."

I clear my throat.
There is more
I know I should say,
but like smoke
from the furnace,
the boys are quickly gone.

What did I expect?

Surprise?
A joyous celebration?
A word of thanks?
Of course not.
They saw freedom coming.
They already knew.

I turn and walk
back up the hill.
This moment
does not
in any way
belong to me.

A New Name

DAVE, 1865

So long,
so long
I have dreamed of this day.
Now it comes
and my heart is numb.
The others are cheering,
cooking,
making plans.
I am an old man
with no place to go —
a potter with one leg.
But I will be
a man with one name
no more.
I have worked for Lewis Miles
for so many years.
My second name could be Miles,
Dave, David Miles.
What about Drake?
Master Drake
taught me to turn a pot
and turn a phrase.
And the famous explorer
Sir Francis Drake,
that was his name too.
I have decided.

From now on
I am David Drake,
potter, poet.
What a sound!
David Drake,
David Drake
indeed.

To a Friend

DAVID DRAKE, 1866

Go on the road,
a one-legged old man
like me?
No, my friend.
But I beg you,
please,
wherever you go,
look for my loved ones.
Look for Eliza,
a skinny girl
with bright eyes.
And look for Lydia,
heavyset and strong,
and her boys, John and George.
Those boys must have children
of their own
by now.
And if you find them,
tell them Dave
is here,
in Edgefield,
waiting.

Little David

DAVID DRAKE, 1870

I'm close to seventy.
That's a long time
for anyone to live.
See over there;
that young boy
is little David,
named for me
because his mama says
he has long fingers —
potter hands!
I say those hands
are made for writing.
But there's no reason
a person can't do both,
now is there?

Come here, David.
Give me that stick
and let me show you
in this dirt
how to write a *D*.
D — that's the first letter
for David —
your name,
mine too, you know.
And when you're bigger

you can write words,
poems too.
You can write whole books!
And I'll teach you
to make pots
on the wheel.
Listen, David.
Your mama's calling.
And me,
I'm going over to the turning house
to see what kind of jar
I will make
today.

AFTERWORD

In a quiet and an unusual way, Dave rebelled against the horror that was slavery. Despite the laws prohibiting slave literacy in South Carolina, Dave wrote words and poems on the walls of his jars, and he often signed his pots with his name and the date. He knew, of course, that everyone could identify the words as his. He also knew he could be severely beaten, maimed, or even killed for defying the law of the land. Still, he was not deterred. Perhaps his skill as a potter gave him confidence. If his hands were cut off, who would make the huge jars and jugs that were so valued for storing meat, lard, pickles, and other foodstuffs? Dave must have felt he could not live without expressing his feelings, his story, and his humanity.

The first period after the end of the Civil War in 1865 was a time of hope for all the people who had been enslaved. But the relationship between the emancipated blacks and their former white owners quickly became confusing. It was hard for both sides to adjust to their new lives and changed society. Hopes were raised among the black men and women by news that the government would provide each family with forty acres of land and a mule as compensation for years of unpaid labor, but the arrangement never materialized. Some former slaves continued to work for the people who had once owned them. Others moved around the country in search of their families and of better life conditions.

After the war, the Union required that Southern states allow all those who were eligible to register to vote. This was a milestone for black men, who went to the polls in large numbers. The registry of Edgefield County, South Carolina, lists David Drake as a registered voter in August 1867. In 1868, these new voters exercised their rights, and many black legislators were elected to the House of Representatives and to the Senate.

Also in 1868, the Ku Klux Klan began to infiltrate Edgefield. Black men and women were attacked, beaten, and sometimes killed in a targeted plan to silence those who were gaining social power. The Klan grew in numbers and strength. Its members terrorized black communities all over South Carolina. In 1871, Congress passed an act that authorized President Grant to use force to remove the Klan from the state, but this act was largely ineffective.

Historians believe that Dave continued to make pottery to support himself after he gained his freedom; but he did not inscribe his name, dates, or any poems on his pots, jugs, and jars. There are also some indications that Dave actually hid his ability to read and write. He may have felt he would be less of a target to members of the Ku Klux Klan and other racist groups if he concealed his education and intelligence.

Dave was a man of extraordinary talent, courage, and wit. He is thought to have died in the late 1870s, when he was close to eighty years old. Very little is known about the last few years of his life. It is possible that Dave's grave was marked with shards from his own pots, which have since disappeared into the soil and clay of South Carolina.

EDGEFIELD POTTERY

The Edgefield district of South Carolina in the early 1800s contained all the resources necessary for the creation of stoneware: pottery that is watertight, strong, and fired at a high temperature. There were abundant deposits of red clay and fine white clay called kaolin near the many streams that run through the area. There was plenty of sand and wood, which were also used in pottery production. And there was slave labor readily available to dig the clay and produce the pottery. However, Edgefield became famous for its stoneware primarily because of the alkaline glazes developed by Dr. Abner Landrum. Prior to the use of alkaline glazes, most glazes in the United States were made of either lead, which was found to be poisonous, or salt, which was very expensive at the time. Dr. Landrum's glazes were made of wood ash, sand, clay, and water. No one is sure exactly how he generated his glaze recipes. He may have read about the materials used to glaze porcelain in ancient China and then, motivated by a desire to run a successful pottery business, he experimented with similar local ingredients. Dr. Landrum's glazes turned out to be safe and affordable. They became one of the outstanding characteristics of Edgefield pottery.

Edgefield pottery was produced from the early 1800s to the early 1900s. It is believed that Dave created thousands of pieces during his lifetime, but only about one hundred seventy of his vessels survive today in museum and private collections. Dave's pots, jugs, and jars were notable for their excellent craftsmanship. Many were also exceptionally large and strong, and some bore intriguing inscriptions, including about thirty poems. Because much of Edgefield pottery was made before the Civil War by enslaved workers in plantation-based pottery works, it has historical and social significance in addition to cultural and artistic importance.

inscription: jar height: 25⅝"
when you fill this Jar with pork or beef
Scot will be there; to Get a peace, —
April 21, 1858

DAVE'S INSCRIPTIONS

Some of Dave's words and poems are included throughout this book to help give readers a sense of his language and an understanding of his thoughts and experiences. The transcriptions of the writings come from *Carolina Clay: The Life and Legend of the Slave Potter Dave* by Leonard Todd, and they follow Dave's spelling, capitalization, and punctuation as closely as possible. Here are Dave's inscriptions that appear in this book.

Concatination
> June 12, 1834

put every bit all between
surely this Jar will hold 14
> July 12, 1834

horses mules and hogs —
all our cows is in the bogs —
there they shall ever stay
till the buzzards take them away =
> March 29, 1836

Dave belongs to Mr Miles /
wher the oven bakes & the pot biles ///
> July 13, 1840

L. Miles   Dave
> October 13, 1843

just a mammouth Jar [illegible]
for I not [illegible]
> October 17, 1850

Lm says this handle
will crack
> June 28, 1854

I wonder where is all my relation
friendship to all — and, every nation
> August 16, 1857

This noble jar = will hold, 20
fill it with silver = then you'll have plenty
> April 8, 1858

Great & Noble Jar
hold Sheep goat or bear
> May 13, 1859

I, made this Jar, all of cross
If, you dont repent, you will be, lost =
> May 3, 1862

AUTHOR'S NOTE

I first heard about Dave while listening to a review of Leonard Todd's book *Carolina Clay: The Life and Legend of the Slave Potter Dave*. After reading the book, I was deeply moved by the story of Dave's life. I had learned about the heroism of people throughout history who had risked their lives for freedom. I was especially interested in Harriet Tubman and Nat Turner. But I had never heard of a person such as Dave. How did he dare to write on the walls of his jars at a time when he could have been whipped or maimed just for reading a book?

Dave's story touched me for many reasons. I grew up in the 1960s, a white girl in a predominantly African American neighborhood in Cincinnati, a city that was full of racial conflict. I remember sitting in the front yard with my friends, most of whom were African American, and hearing the sounds of the 1968 race riots just a few blocks away. Perhaps because of these early experiences I am deeply interested in struggles for civil rights around the world. My children, who are biracial Chinese and Caucasian, have grown up in this same neighborhood and have also been significantly affected by issues of race and class.

I have a connection to Dave's love of clay as well. As a child, my friends and I spent hot summer days in the basement of the neighborhood community center. The center had a big vat of red clay, and from that clay we formed sculptures and pots. I learned to slice and wedge the clay so it would hold up when fired in the kiln, or furnace. I practiced centering a mound of clay on a potter's wheel. I came to love the feeling of clay in my hands. This interest was passed on to one of my children, Ann, who is now an avid potter.

Like Dave, I also write poetry. I started writing poems when I was about eight, and I have been writing poetry — and prose — ever since. I was encouraged by teachers, family members, and friends. I cannot imagine writing at all in the circumstances under which Dave lived and worked.

I have told Dave's story in a way that I hope he would have liked: in poems and woodcuts that attempt to communicate his bravery, his dignity, and his artistry. In some small way, I hope to pay tribute to the quiet heroism of David Drake.

ACKNOWLEDGMENTS

I am very grateful to Leonard Todd, author of *Carolina Clay: The Life and Legend of the Slave Potter Dave*, for helping me so much with this project. He met me in Edgefield, South Carolina, to show me the places that were important in Dave's life — where Dave lived, worked, and died. Mr. Todd was very generous with his time and expertise. Thank you also to Stephen Ferrell, resident potter at Old Edgefield Pottery, who showed me the work in his studio, including a pot signed by Dave.

Additional thanks to the following people who reviewed the manuscript for this book and offered their valuable input: Dr. Pauletta Brown Bracy, School of Library and Information Sciences, North Carolina Central University; Jill Beute Koverman, Chief Curator of Collections and Research, McKissick Museum, University of South Carolina; Emily Alyssa Owens, Doctoral Student in African American Studies and History, Harvard University; and Dr. Freddie L. Parker, Professor of History, North Carolina Central University.

AUTHOR'S SOURCES

Baldwin, Cinda K. *Great & Noble Jar: Traditional Stoneware of South Carolina*. Athens: University of George Press, 1993.

Burrison, John A. *Brothers in Clay: The Story of Georgia Folk Pottery*. Athens: University of Georgia Press, 1983.

"Edgefield District Pottery: Origins of Southern Stoneware." *SCIWAY News*, October 2008. SCIWAY: South Carolina's Information Highway. http://www.sciway.net/south-carolina/edgefield-district-pottery.html.

Federal Writers' Project, comp. *Georgia Slave Narratives*. Carlisle, MA: Applewood Books, 2006.
———. *South Carolina Slave Narratives*. Carlisle, MA: Applewood Books, 2006.

Goldberg, Arthur F., and James P. Witkowski. "Beneath His Magic Touch: The Dated Vessels of the African-American Slave Potter Dave." Robert Hunter, ed. *Ceramics in America 2006*: 58–92.

Koverman, Jill Beute, ed. *I Made This Jar: The Life and Works of the Enslaved African-American Potter, Dave*. Columbia, SC: McKissick Museum, University of South Carolina, 1998.

Pottery, Poetry, and Politics Surrounding the Enslaved African-American Potter, Dave. Columbia, SC: McKissick Museum, University of South Carolina, 1998.

Reif, Rita. "In a Slave's Pottery, a Saga of Courage and Beauty." *New York Times*, Arts section, January 30, 2000.

Todd, Leonard. *Carolina Clay: The Life and Legend of the Slave Potter Dave.* New York, W. W. Norton & Company, 2008.

———. Interviews and informal tour with the author. Edgefield area, SC: April 19 and 20, 2010.